DUCK
GETS A JOB

Sonny Ross

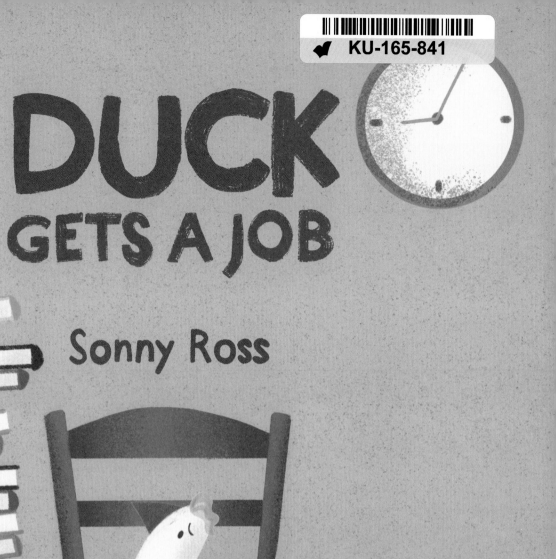

This is Duck.
Duck wants a job.

All of Duck's friends worked in the city
and they just never stopped going on about it.

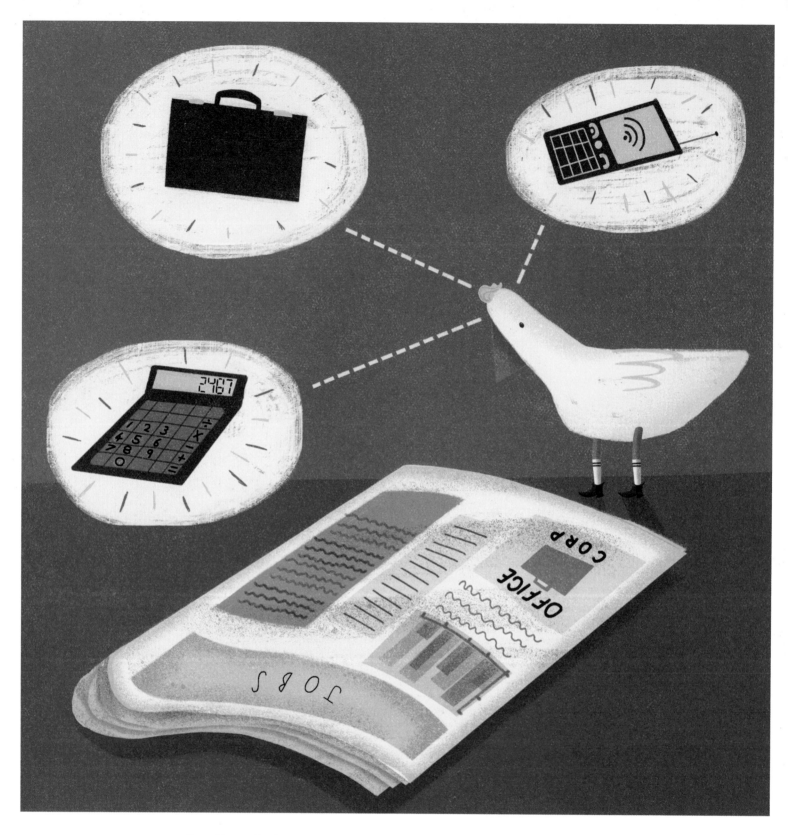

So Duck looked at the adverts for city jobs.
They seemed like boring jobs for a duck,
but he picked one anyway. And he got an interview!

He couldn't decide what to wear to the job interview.
He didn't want to make a bad first impression.
He opted for the Professional Look.

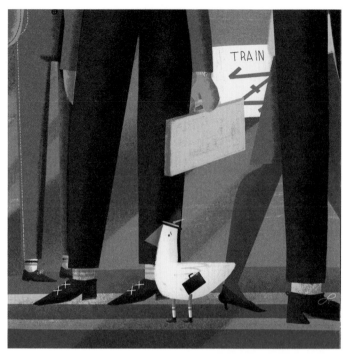

Next Duck had to decide how to get there.
Public transport is tricky for ducks,
and flying would make him tired and scruffy.

He chose to walk.

He got lost.

When Duck finally arrived in the city,
he had to get a taxi so he wouldn't be late.

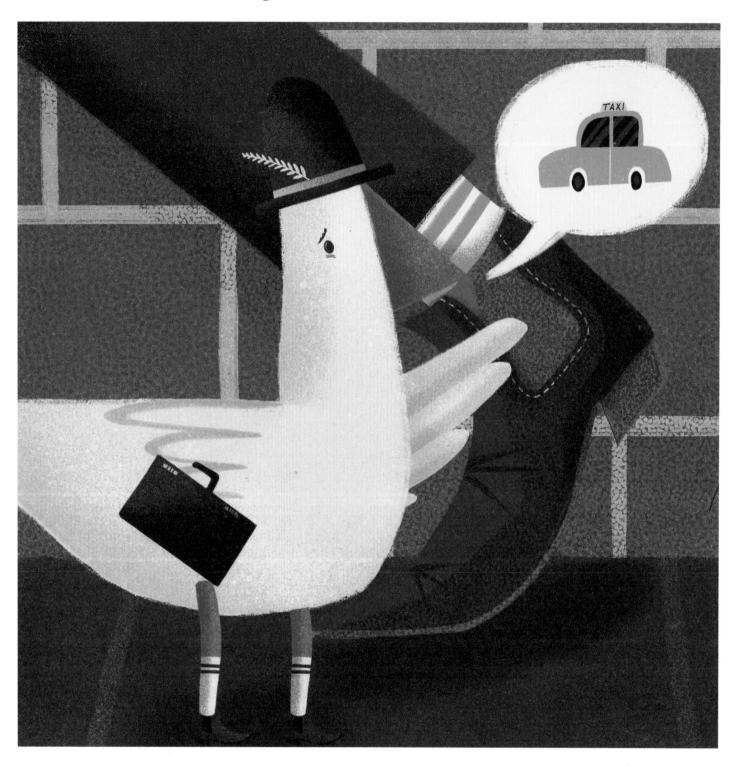

In the taxi he thought about how he should
behave at the interview.

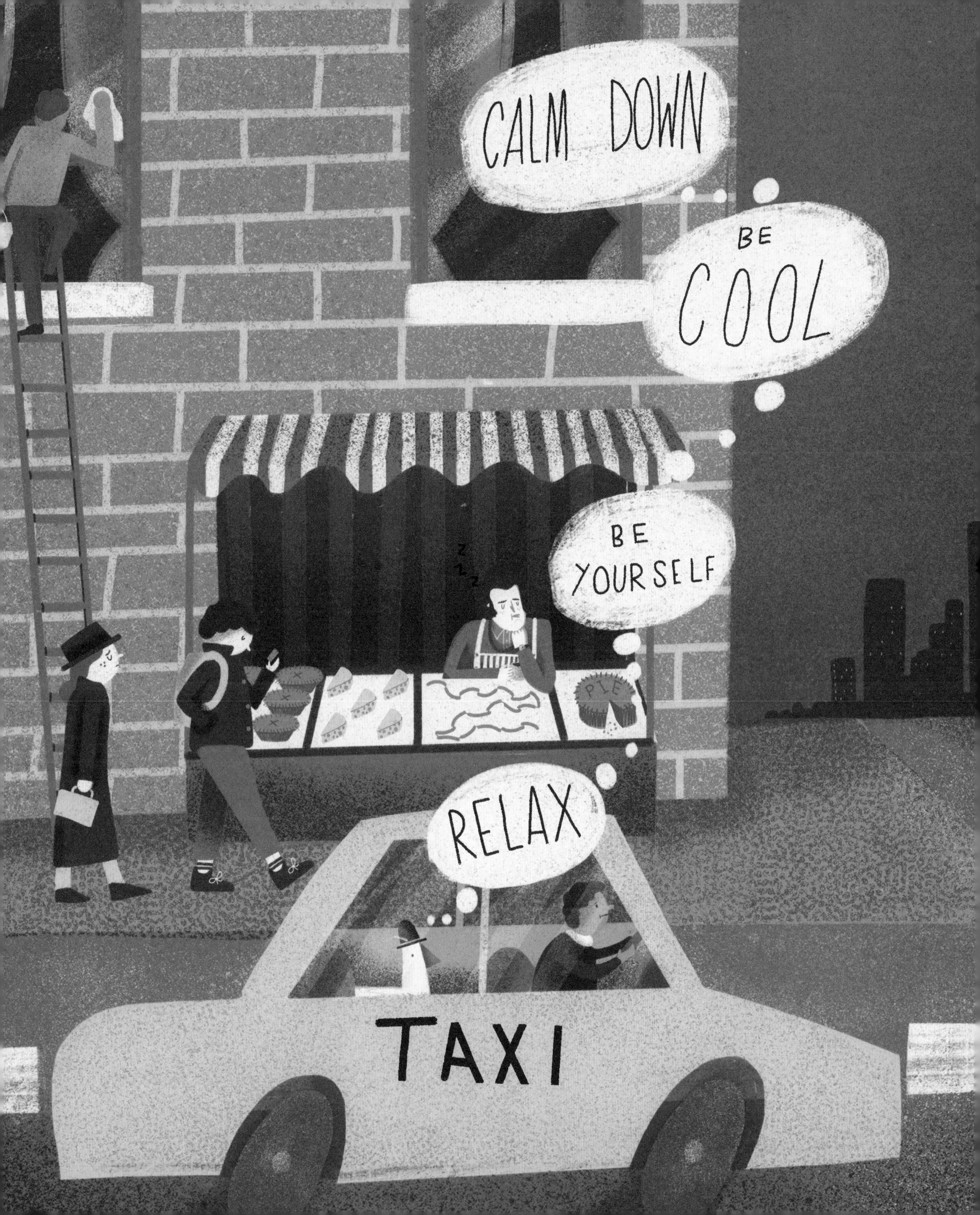
CALM DOWN
BE COOL
BE YOURSELF
PIE
RELAX
TAXI

Because he couldn't decide, Duck wasn't cool,
professional or relaxed. He was very nervous.

But he got the job!

Duck soon realised that spreadsheets full of facts
and figures did not interest him at all.

And right after his nap he would finally make up his own mind
about what *he* wanted . . .

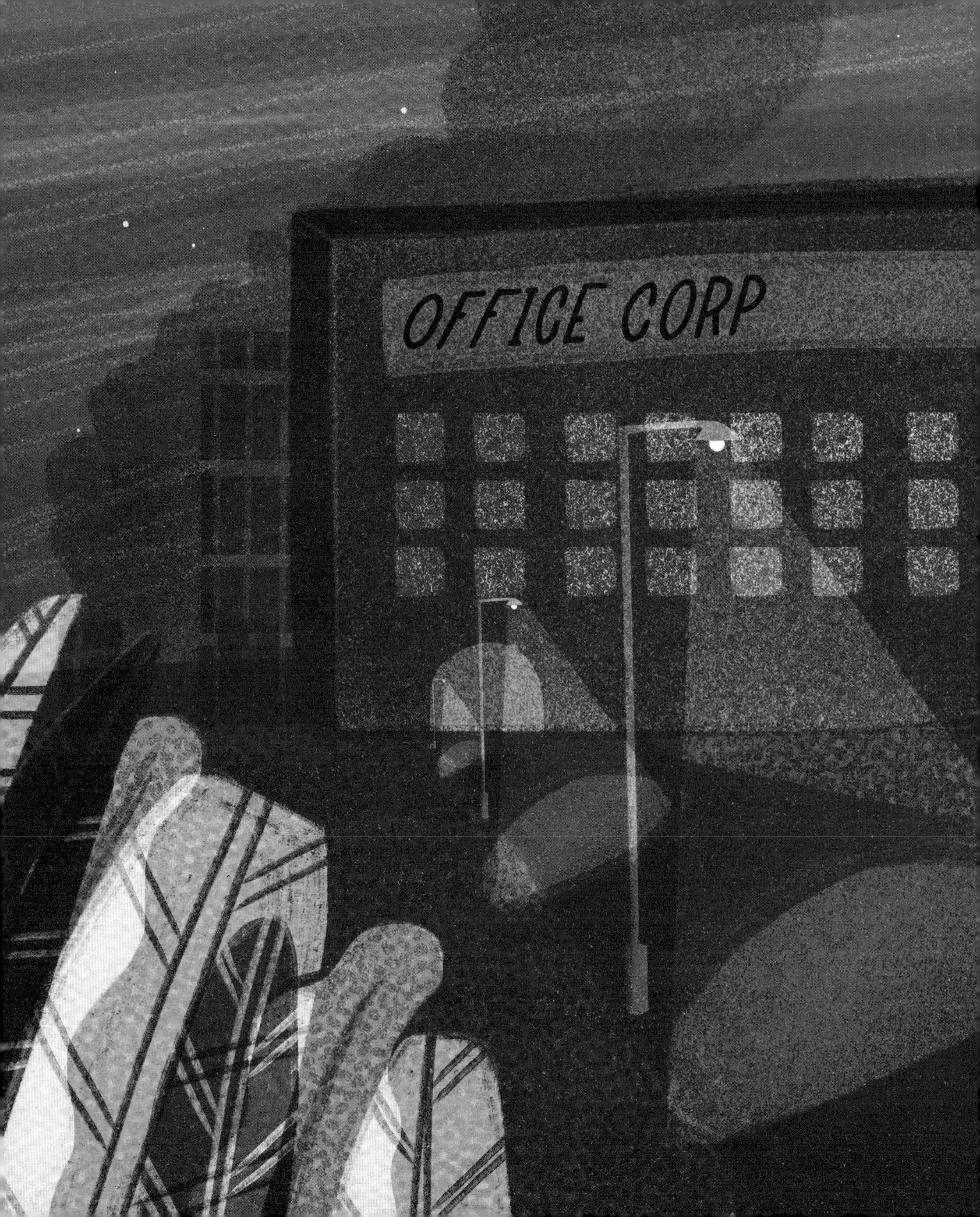
OFFICE CORP

Duck decided to quit.

He had always wanted to be an artist.
He'd studied all the famous painters.

This time, Duck found a job that better suited
him and his interests.

He put samples of his best work in a portfolio, and
decided to relax and be himself at the interview.

He checked his route to make sure he didn't get lost, and
he left plenty of time so he wouldn't be late.

He showed his work and he wasn't nervous at all.
He felt confident because he was being himself.

Duck got the job!
He was very happy.

Duck loved his new job so much,
he didn't even need an afternoon nap.

Duck's decision to take control of his life had paid off.

Sometimes you just have to be really brave, and follow your dreams.